WHEN THE WIND STOPS

Revised and newly illustrated edition

by Charlotte Zolotow

illustrated by Stefano Vitale

HarperCollins*Publishers*

The great bright yellow sun had shone all day, and now the day was coming to an end. The light in the sky changed from blue to pink to a strange dusky purple. The sun sank lower into the long glowing clouds.

The little boy was sorry to see the day end.

He and his friend had played in the garden.

When they were tired of playing, they lay down in the grass and felt the sun on them, warm and soft, like a sleepy cat resting.

There had been icy lemonade, in the afternoon, which they drank under the pear tree.

And the little boy's father read him a story on the porch before he went to bed.

Now his mother came to say good night.

"Why does the day have to end?" he asked her.

"So night can begin," she said, "look."

She pointed out the window where, high in the darkening sky, behind the branches of the pear tree, the little boy could see a pale sliver of moon.

"That's the night beginning," his mother said, resting her hand on his shoulder, "the night with the moon and stars and darkness for you to dream in."

"But where does the sun go when the day ends?" the little boy asked.

"The day doesn't end," said his mother, "it begins somewhere else. The sun will be shining there, when night begins here. Nothing ends."

"Nothing?" the little boy asked.

"Nothing," his mother said. "It begins in another place or in a different way."

The little boy lay in bed, and his mother sat beside him.

"Where does the wind go when it stops?" he asked.

"It blows away to make the trees dance somewhere else."

"Where does the dandelion fluff go

when it blows away?"

"It carries the seed of new dandelions

to someone's lawn."

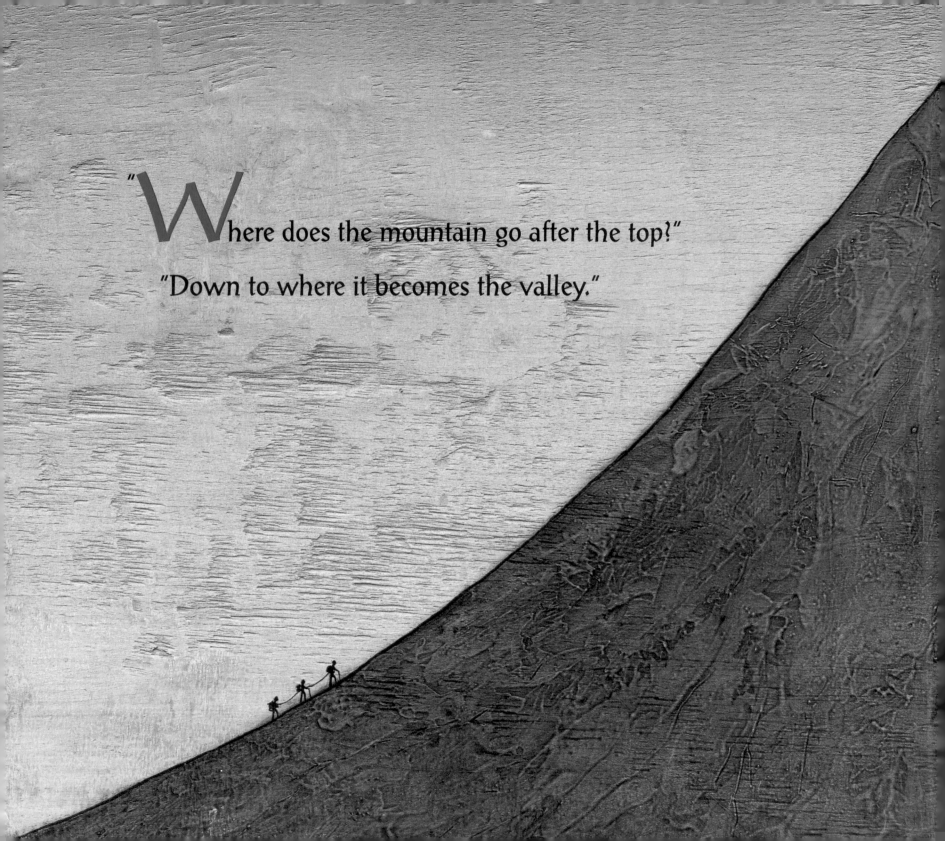

"Where does the mountain go after the top?"

"Down to where it becomes the valley."

"Where do waves go when they break on the sand?"

"Sucked back to the sea into new waves."

"Where does the rain go

when the storm is over?"

"Into clouds to make other storms."

"And where do clouds go when they move
across the sky?"

"To make shade somewhere else."

"And the leaves in the forest

when they turn color and fall?"

"Into the ground to become part of new trees

with new leaves."

"But when the leaves fall, that is the end of something!" the little boy said. "It is the end of autumn."

"Yes," his mother said. "The end of autumn is when the winter begins."

"And the end of winter . . . ?" the little boy asked.

"The end of winter, when the snow melts and the birds come back, is the beginning of spring," his mother said.

The little boy smiled.

"It really does go on and on," he said.

"Nothing ends."

He looked out at the sky. The sun was gone completely. The lovely pink clouds had disappeared. The sky was dark and purple-black. High above the branches of the pear tree shone, clearly now, a thin new moon.

"Today is over," his mother said. "It's time for sleep,

and tomorrow morning, when you wake,

the moon will be beginning a night far away,

and the sun will be here to begin a new day."

To Ned Shank, with love—
Charlotte

For Robert O. Warren
S.V.

When the Wind Stops   Text copyright © 1962, 1995 by Charlotte Zolotow.   Text copyright
renewed 1990 by Charlotte Zolotow.   Illustrations copyright © 1995 by Stefano Vitale.
Printed in Mexico. All rights reserved.   Library of Congress Cataloging-in-Publication
Data   Zolotow, Charlotte, date   When the wind stops / by Charlotte Zolotow ; illustrated
by Stefano Vitale.—Rev. and newly illustrated ed.   p.   cm.   Summary: A mother
explains to her son that in nature an end is also a beginning as day gives way to night,
winter ends and spring begins, and, after it stops falling, rain makes clouds for other storms.
ISBN 0-06-026971-5. — ISBN 0-06-096972-3 (lib. bdg.) — ISBN 0-06-443472-9 (pbk.)
[1. Nature—Fiction.]   I. Vitale, Stefano, ill.   II. Title. PZ7.Z77Wgj   1995   [E]—dc20
94-14477   CIP   AC Typography by Al Cetta   ❖   Revised and Newly Illustrated Edition